Harriet

Written by

Barbara Townsend

illustrated by Chantal Bourgonje

Second edition published by Savernake Press 2017
First edition published by Savernake Press 2014

ISBN: 978-0-9957039-1-9

Savernake Press, Burbage, Wiltshire SN8 3AN

Website:- www.savernakepress.weebly.com

e-mail:- babstownsend@hotmail.com

Illustrated in Wiltshire by Chantal Marie Bourgonje. www.cfordesign.co.uk

Printed locally by Bulpitt Print Ltd on paper, that is fully recyclable, biodegradable and contains fibre from forests meeting the Forest Stewardship Council principles and criteria (FSC).

Preface

Although deviating slightly from the facts for the purpose of Harriet's story, I hope, it does not affect your enjoyment of her journey.

A Honey Bee

This busy creature is very small
If she didn't hum, we wouldn't notice her at all
Her role is vital, so important to us
Be glad she is so industrious
So plant many seeds so she can feed
Do remember she also needs weeds

Barbara Townsend 2014

Acknowledgements

This book was wonderful to research and a pleasure to write. All made possible with the help from the following people. A massive thank you to:-

Wiltshire Beekeepers Association (WBKA):
For your guidance on factual content.

Joy:
For editing and your patience.

Ebony (age 11) and Grace (age 7):
Thank you for listening and giving such useful comments.

Chantal Bourgonje:
Thank you for the beautiful illustrations that have once again brought my stories to life.

My Granddaughter Issy (age 10):

Thank you again for reading my stories and giving such good advice. I am always eager to learn.

My family:

Thank you for your support and encouragement.

Last but not least. My Husband Ian:

I could not do this without your unwavering belief in me. I love you.

CONTENTS

Harriet

Hidden from predators high above the forest floor in an ancient oak tree, a large colony of bees remained undetected for several years. The nest had become worn and ragged. Thousands of bees entering and leaving on their daily forays had left their mark. The ancient oak, it too showing its age, had become gnarly, with deep dark crevices etched into the length of its ageing rugged trunk.

The tree had thickened; its wild limbs reached skywards with sprawling distorted branches that twisted endlessly outwards and upwards. A large hollow had developed where one of the tree's withered branches had fallen during a winter's storm. A perfect location, that provided protection from the elements and good ventilation on hot days.

The resident Queen had carefully selected this site. As an intelligent bee, she had invested her time and energy in selecting a nest site that would not only provide a safe environment for the rearing of her offspring, but would benefit future generations.

Harriet belonged to this 30,000 strong colony. With glossy gold and bold stripes and very long antennae made this large healthy honeybee appear even bigger.

Her translucent wings, although small, worked hard to keep her airborne; she could beat them up to 11,000 times per minute, making each beat impossible to see through the blurred movements. Harriet looked clumsy flying. However, despite her size and awkwardness, she could avoid obstacles with great skill.

Harriet knew numerous bees she worked with and met day to day but she could by no means know the thousands that lived within her colony. Harriet instinctively recognised a bee, by the manner of its flight or by its scent, like a sixth sense. The Queen's energy, it too so powerful, would radiate throughout the entire colony, a force that affected them all. Harriet certainly didn't understand it, something unseen, a force unexplained, something which no bee questioned, except for Harriet. Daily life in the colony varied little. The bees carried out their duties without question. As Harriet carried out her tasks, she would watch the others, always amazed how it all worked.

One morning as the clouds scuttled across the sky on a very cold, grey and wet day, a group of worker bees were grumbling. "It's raining," they moaned.

"That's great," said Harriet happily. She hated the rain as much as they did but always remained positive. They all raced back to the nest not wanting to get wet.

Harriet, always happy, would cheerfully carry out her duties. In general bees liked her, they would seek out her company and she would greet them warmly, always happy to spend time with them.

Harriet spent most days working with a group of female bees, collecting pollen and nectar. She liked these bees. They were friendly and they would gather at the entrance to the nest catching up on the day's events and happenings. They would point out to each other, the direction to the best plants and flowers. This was a good spot to pass on vital information.

"The pollen is so good today," said one bee.

"I've collected so much my wings feel tired from all the trips back to the nest," said another.

The collection of pollen to Harriet seemed to happen by accident. As the bees collected nectar, pollen would stick to their bodies covering them in coloured grains. The bees would transfer the grains from their bodies to pollen baskets located on their back legs, where they could carry it before returning to the nest to store it in cells.

The bees would make numerous trips in one day to offload the pollen. The summer months were a tiring time for them all. Harriet had seen many bees so loaded and weighted down with the pollen it looked difficult for them to fly.

"Hey," said one of the bees, "did you see the young bees over there by the brambles?" she continued chattily. "They didn't have a clue what they were doing. They were flying into one another, rushing around in circles not knowing which way to fly home."

"Let's help them tomorrow," said Harriet, "they're young and still have a lot to learn."

"There she goes again," the bee grumbled. "You're always helping others and getting them out of trouble. When do they ever return the favour?"

"I'm not bothered about that," said Harriet, "I like helping. Besides, the quicker they learn the more pollen they will collect. That's a good thing, isn't it?"

"I guess so," said the bee, trying not to appear too mean.

They all worked late into the afternoon, taking advantage of the sunny day and the plentiful pollen.

"Come on you lot," shouted Harriet. "Time we were getting back. It's getting dark and we still have to get this pollen back to the stores."

The group flew off and raced back to the colony. Harriet always arrived home before the others, much to their annoyance; she could fly fast despite her size.

The Storm

The day had been hot and steamy and they were all suffering from the intense heat. Several bees were frantically flapping their wings positioned in appropriate places around the nest trying to keep it cool.

The distant thunder rumbled all that day. However, the dark, threatening, billowing clouds had kept their distance; an ominous dark line crept across the horizon. As the day heated up, the wind changed, pushing the clouds closer and closer.

Suddenly the storm hit. Although not exciting, it created a deviation from their normal everyday lives.

The air became stifling and the sky darkened with the black, thunderous clouds, which were now overhead. Streaks of lightning flashed across the sky, lighting up the dark, menacing clouds. The deafening thunder shook the very core of the tree, vibrating deep within the nest.

The wind, so strong, blew the rain horizontally into the entrance, completely saturating everything. The deluge of rain created rivulets, which ran throughout the nest and chambers, endangering the young, eggs and food, all of which were stored in hexagonal shaped wax cells, produced by many of the younger bees.

Using wax from little glands on the underside of their bodies they would take the wax in their mouths, chew it before applying it to the nest creating these amazing shapes.

As the rain poured down, the bees returned to the colony like a well-trained army. In an instant, they set to work, blocking leaks and protecting the young, shielding the eggs and food from the worst of the water.

Then, as the storm subsided and the rain slowed, the bees again, in a military fashion, systematically cleared the water to dry out the nest. All completed without a word or a command from anyone. Instinctively they all knew what to do and just did it.

Once the danger had passed and the nest safe and dry, like a switch, they all returned to their normal tasks as though nothing had happened. This intrigued and puzzled Harriet.

With so much activity within the colony, the nest required constant repairs. Various bees would collect tree sap and would turn it into a gluey substance; they would use this to cement damaged chambers and glue bits together. The bees would get extremely sticky.

Harriet found it funny watching them trying to unglue themselves; their bodies slicked smooth with the goo.

Changes

Flying busily from flower to flower, the sound of bees feeding and collecting their daily quota filled the air. The hot summer sun had shone brightly for days and the pollen and nectar became plentiful.

The bees were industrious. Working long hours late into the evenings, carrying vast quantities of nectar and pollen back to the colony and only resting once the sun had gone down.

Harriet would often watch as the bees flew out from the nest in search of nectar-rich flowers for honey production. To turn nectar into honey required teamwork. The bees would gorge on the nectar and would return once their stomachs were full.

Once back in the nest they would regurgitate the nectar fluid and give it to the nest workers. The workers would eat the sugary nectar. Harriet knew that in doing this, it somehow changed it. They would then in turn regurgitate the transformed nectar, depositing it into the wax cells for storage. Overtime the sugary substance would thicken into honey and the nest bees would cap the cells with wax, sealing the honey into the honeycomb.

Working as a team, the thousands of worker bees in Harriet's colony could produce plenty of honey for all of them. Harriet rarely went hungry.

"The winter will be good this year," said Harriet. "Our stores of honey should see us through until late spring. That will give the young ones a fantastic start," she said happily.

"She's at it again," said a group of bees. "Such a goody goody," they sneered mockingly. Harriet had noticed that recently, these bees had become bad tempered and constantly complaining. Harriet would acknowledge and greet them; though not wanting to ruffle their feathers or anger them, she would keep her distance.

Although some of the bees could be grumpy from time to time, Harriet always thought how gentle and caring most bees could be, especially to the young ones as they emerged from their egg chambers. Harriet had watched as the bees mixed honey with pollen to make beebread and fed this special food to the young whilst still at their larvae stage.

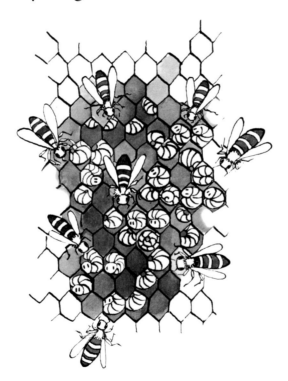

A few select youngsters, however, were lucky and fed royal jelly. This wonderful substance would have a profound effect on their life and existence within the colony.

Certain bees produced it from special glands on their heads. Harriet had watched as the bees gently and carefully fed this jelly to the young. She could remember the delicious taste of the warm sticky substance.

The grumbling and bad behaviour by some of the bees became frequent and worried Harriet. An unsettling sense of danger crept through Harriet's mind.

This particular day, they appeared to be looking for trouble. Harriet had seen this group pushing their weight around before, especially picking on the younger bees that were an easy target for the bullying bees.

They stared menacingly at Harriet and she instinctively knew there would be trouble.

There were six of them and as she quickly looked around she realised she was completely on her own.

Suddenly, and without warning, they flew hard and fast straight at Harriet, grabbing her tightly and slamming her into the ground. "Where do you think you're going?" the biggest of the group said, growling at her.

"Collecting pollen, as you should be," she said, breathless and terrified. Harriet had hit the ground hard; they all held her down, flattening and pushing her into the wet earth. "Please let me go," she said through her pain, finding it hard to breathe.

Despite being a strong bee and desperate to get away, she could not defend herself or reason against six of them.

Suddenly and unexpectedly, Harriet became aware of anger growing within her. Living as part of a colony, she had never experienced that feeling before; there hadn't been situations where she needed to be angry. Many of the bees had begun behaving in ways that were alien to her. She had noticed the behaviour on several occasions but dismissed it as overzealous play by the younger bees.

As anger grew within her, so did her strength. With rage intensifying and fear subsiding, Harriet suddenly heaved the bees aside and yelled, "ENOUGH!" Something changed in that moment.

The stunned bees could feel it and so could Harriet. As if being pushed back by unseen force, the bees backed away. They could sense the strength and power radiating from Harriet. Confused and humiliated, they took flight back to the colony, not daring to look back.

Harriet remained on the ground, shocked and bewildered at what had happened. "I don't understand," Harriet said aloud. "Why would they listen to me?"

Harriet shook her head in disbelief and headed home.

Eventually, the situation in the colony became intolerable. The fighting and bullying became widespread. Many of the bees were frightened to venture outside. They would feed on the stored honey rather than run the risk of an attack by one of their own.

The nest began to look shabby and disorganised. The nursery, which lay deep inside the nest, was occasionally unguarded, putting the eggs and young at risk. The collection of water droplets placed around the nest to control the temperature had stopped. The remaining droplets were drying up.

The bees didn't seem to care or be concerned; they looked confused and unsure what to do. A number of bees were diligently using their wings to fan the cool air generated by the water, but were unaware that it had already evaporated.

Only a few industrious braver individuals would venture outside. The rest would argue, fight and feed on the stored honey, now running dangerously low. There wouldn't be enough food to see them through the winter if this continued.

Harriet became increasingly troubled about how their lives were changing. Many of the bees didn't notice, unless they were on the receiving end of one of the many bullies. They would look bewildered and scared after a beating from one of the marauding groups and would then carry on as though nothing had happened. "What is happening to us?" she muttered aloud. "What can I do? How can I stop them? They don't seem to care. They're not asking questions. They're accepting the fighting and bullying. WHY BEHAVE THIS WAY?" she screamed.

Harriet became increasingly frustrated and the anger she felt when she'd been attacked, slowly crept back. That unseen controlling force that ruled their everyday lives began losing its grip, slowly disappearing and Harriet knew it.

The Attack

They came in droves. The attack, sudden and well executed. It was as though the hornets had waited and watched as the colony became unprotected, chaotic and vulnerable.

The hornets were large and mean and were determined to decimate the colony. With a deadly focus, their aim to feed their growing young with stolen honey and eggs drove them forward. The hornets would slay any bee that stood in their way.

As their menacing hum grew louder, Harriet's colony panicked. With lack of leadership and completely out of control, the confused bees flew in all directions pursued by the hornets. "THEY DON'T STAND A CHANCE!" Harriet screamed.

An instinct to survive overwhelmed Harriet, for herself but also for the others.

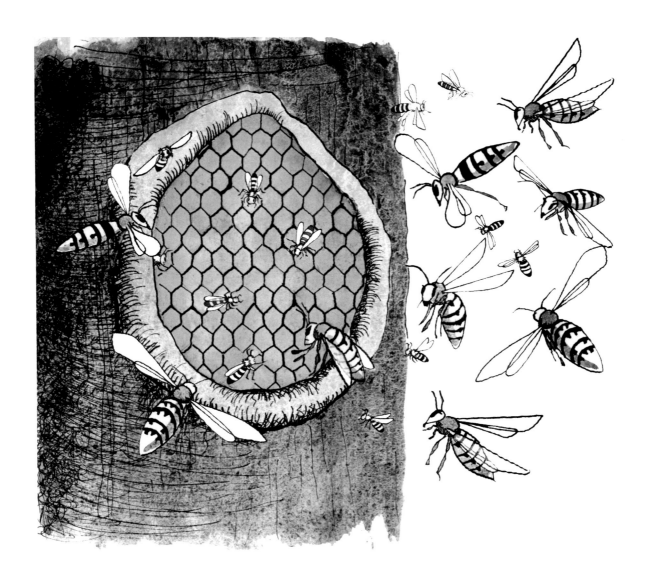

With her anger came her strength. "FOLLOW ME!" she bellowed. Those bees not pursued by hornets came and followed her; they did not question.

Harriet flew hard and fast in an unknown direction. She knew she needed to get to safety and as far away as possible from the deadly hornets.

The bees followed, many still in shock from the attack. They flew on and on, tirelessly and endlessly and Harriet knew that they would eventually need to rest and feed or they would become too exhausted to continue.

She needed to be sure they were safe and no longer followed. As they flew on, Harriet scanned the surrounding area for a suitable place to rest; she had to make a quick decision.

In a clearing at the edge of a small wood, she spotted a patch of wild flowers and thistles. "We could rest by the trees and feed," she said to herself quietly. Luckily, the area seemed remote and quiet; there were a few unknown bees feeding and collecting pollen, but they were far too busy to notice the unfamiliar visitors.

Harriet quickly found a small opening high in a tree and the others followed her inside. "Rest for a while and then go off and feed. Stay in small groups but keep close together," she said reassuringly but firmly. Somehow, she knew she had to keep them under control. They obeyed Harriet's orders with a silent relief.

Harriet too flew off to feed to regain her strength, relieved to be alone to have a few moments without the responsibility of the others. "I must find a suitable site for a new home," she muttered.

She knew they couldn't return to their nest. Even if the hornets had gone, they could return at any time, as they now knew the exact location. It would be foolish and dangerous. She could sense the urgency within her.

While Harriet fed, her strength returned. She watched as the wild flowers blew gently in the breeze and she knew an extraordinary connection existed between her, the colony and the plants.

Harriet had always been observant. She knew that when the plants and flowers were at their very best, plentiful and healthy, her colony would thrive and produce more young. There would, however, always be plenty of pollen and nectar to support the hungry new mouths.

After the attack and the decimation of her colony, Harriet became fearful that this cycle and unique connection would break down.

"What if what has happened to us is happening to other colonies? Surely, that would mean fewer bees, which would mean fewer flowers and plants next season. How would we feed ourselves? How would we survive?" Her troubled thoughts raced.

The Journey

After feeding for a short while, Harriet felt stronger and headed back to where she had left the others. As she approached the tree, she could see them busily flying around the entrance to the hollow. As she entered, she could see they were attempting to build a nest.

Having fed, they too were obviously feeling refreshed and their instinct to build too strong for them not to. "NOT HERE!" she ordered. They stopped immediately and waited for her guidance.

She knew the site to be unsuitable. It just didn't feel right. They needed to move on quickly. They followed her in a tight formation, again, without question.

As the days passed, she led the group from feeding areas to safe places to rest. Their days became a constant battle to survive and the strain began taking its toll. Harriet had to abandon those who could not keep up.

To stop could endanger the others. The urgency to find a new home panicked her. How long could she keep this up and what would happen if she couldn't find a safe place for them?

Then, on a bright clear morning, as she led the group once again, she spotted a forest ahead, a vast area that bordered a bright sunny meadow. The forest stretched out as far as she could see. Harriet immediately headed for the trees. As they flew closer, she noticed a carpet of colourful wild flowers, which covered the meadow, such a welcoming sight.

As they approached, she could see trees that were familiar to her, mainly beech and oak; various trees were tall and thin, many were squat and very wide. "This is it, this is the place," she said excitely. "This feels right."

"Come on, stay together," she ordered. Harriet headed for a large strong, stout oak tree; its trunk had grown wide and gnarly. Its branches reached high into the sky forming a huge canopy; the tree had fought for its space and now dominated the area around itself. Harriet left the others to rest and began searching the tree for a suitable place to build a nest. High up close to one of the main branches she found an opening, created by an old limb that had torn away by the strong winter winds. "Perfect," she said.

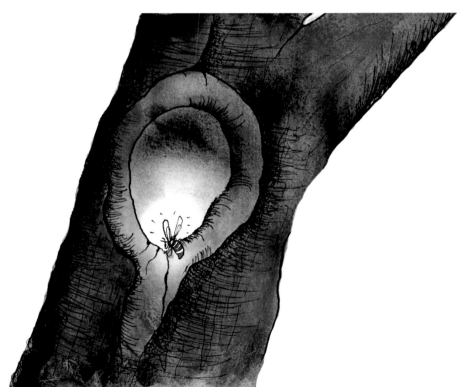

Harriet slowly entered the hollow, aware there could be bees already living inside that would attack her for trespassing. Worst of all, it could be a hornets' nest.

Thankfully empty, she ventured deep into the hollow to investigate its condition and suitability. "There is enough room in here," she whispered. "The opening is facing away from the worst of the weather, it's well ventilated and the entrance is sheltered by the main branch above. This is it," she said calmly.

Coming Home

Harriet flew excitedly back to the others; she now had a sense of relief and the stress she had felt began to subside. "Follow me," she ordered. The group headed to the hollow and instinctively set to work clearing and preparing the site. There were no questions just an eagerness and willingness to build drove them on.

To create a new nest would take time. With an inbuilt skill, they all knew what to do and who would do it.

Large quantities of wax were required to produce the cells to form the nest. Young and older workers immediately began producing the wax, chewing it and making it soft and manageable to create the right shape for the cells.

They began to build a honeycomb that would house young bees and eggs and store honey, nectar and pollen. Crucially they needed to produce and store honey, so that they would be able to feed themselves during the coming winter months. If they failed to stock enough, most of them would not survive the winter.

Harriet felt the urgency to get the colony established to ensure their survival. However, new feelings began to overwhelm her. A force, she had little or no control over. It had a strange comforting and soothing effect.

The nest quickly began to take shape and the bees soon settled into their day-to-day lives of maintaining, collecting, feeding and protecting the colony. Life became normal again.

Harriet though, would occasionally fly off to be by herself and would spend time away from the colony. Now happy and contented, Harriet would watch the bees and sigh with relief. They had come such a long way since the deadly attack by the hornets.

Those that had survived had worked so hard, deserved to be safe and happy.

The site Harriet had chosen, had been perfect, an intelligent choice. The colony now had an opportunity to become well established. There was, however, one vital element still missing. Bees, they needed bees and masses of them.

That soothing and calming feeling Harriet had been experiencing, seemed to wrap itself around her body, it came in slow, gentle waves affecting her whole being.

Now perched at the entrance to their new home, Harriet took one last look around her and slowly, deliberately, headed to the depths of the nest.

As she made her way deeper and further into the darkness, the bees touched her, gently guiding and encouraging her on. They too now understood. She could sense their energy as well as her own.

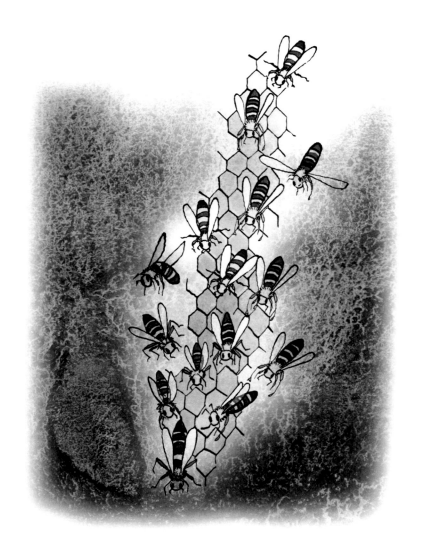

The unseen force that once radiated throughout their old home existed right there in that moment.

Harriet now had an absolute understanding of her role and so did the others. She needed to lay eggs, thousands of them. There was now at last a sense of coming home.

Harriet had become Queen.

Also available:-

Written by Barbara Townsend
Illustrated by Chantal Bourgonje

'The Savernake Big Belly Oak'

As frightened creatures escape into the safety of Tree's enormous big belly, he comforts them with tales of the forest.
For children 4 to 11 years.

'The Oaks of Savernake and the Legendary Ghosts'

Venerable veteran oak trees stand in the ancient forest of Savernake. Over 1000 years old, many have shrunk under their own great weight and have become wide and gnarly, their immense size bending and twisting them out of shape giving them the appearance of demons and monsters.

They are, however, gentle giants with powers far beyond our understanding.

For children 7 to 11 years.

'Stonehenge – Luke and the Bluestone'

Luke, the main character, is a 15 year old school boy, is not keen on the idea of a school trip to 'some old stones'!! With a twist of past and present Luke, is unwittingly placed amongst the very people transporting one of the mighty Bluestones from West Wales to Wiltshire. Travelling with them, they experience some of the emotions and extremes of human effort that must have gone into building one of mankind's singular and most remarkable achievements.

For children 8 to 12 years.

'Old Harry Rock and Tales of the Jurassic Coast'

Old Harry Rock stand sentinel and bravely fends off the sea's attempts to claim him. The surrounding chalk, like a sponge, soaks up visions, myths, legends and stories, storing them as memories in the cliffs and deep within the sea bed, like long lost fossils waiting to be dug up and discovered. Immeasurable amounts of images and sounds create an energy force waiting to be released. Old Harry has powers and can tap into this vast energy resource to save humans and sea creatures in peril. For children 7 to 11 years.

www.savernakepress.weebly.com

babstownsend@hotmail.com